The Littlest DINOSAUR'S BIG Adventure

For Sarah O, with thanks

Bloomsbury Publishing, London, Berlin and New York

First published in Great Britain in 2009 by Bloomsbury Publishing Plc
36 Soho Square, London, W1D 3QY

A CIP catalogue record of this book is available from the British Library

Hardback ISBN 978 0 7475 8983 9

1 3 5 7 9 10 8 6 4 2

Paperback ISBN 978 0 7475 8982 2

1 3 5 7 9 10 8 6 4 2

Printed in China

All papers used by Bloomsbury Publishing are natural, recyclable products
made from wood grown in well-managed forests. The manufacturing processes
conform to the environmental regulations of the country of origin

www.bloomsbury.com/childrens

The Littlest DINOSAUR'S BIG Adventure

MICHAEL FOREMAN

BLOOMSBURY

LONDON BERLIN NEW YORK

The littlest dinosaur sat by the river and dangled his toes among the water lilies.

Suddenly a frog landed on a lily pad
between the littlest dinosaur's feet.

Plip!

Plop!

Flip!

Flop!

The frog hopped to another lily pad and looked back at the littlest dinosaur. Then he hopped to the next lily pad and the next, and looked back at him again.

Carefully, the littlest dinosaur stepped on to the nearest lily pad. It wibbled and wobbled but didn't sink. Then he stepped carefully on to the next. When the frog saw that the littlest dinosaur was following him,

he did a double backflip and clapped his hands.

The littlest dinosaur was suddenly surrounded by frogs somersaulting, hopping and diving among the lilies.

"This is fun!" cried the littlest dinosaur. "At last I have some friends my own size."

He followed the frogs, lily pad by lily pad, across the river.

Splash!

Splish!

When he reached the opposite riverbank, there were wild flowers that stretched as far as he could see. Here there were no big, clumsy dinosaurs to trample them, only bees buzzing and butterflies flitting from flower to flower.

A butterfly landed on the littlest dinosaur's nose and opened its wings.

"How beautiful you are," whispered the littlest dinosaur, and he walked on, surrounded by a cloud of brilliant butterflies.

It's such fun being small, he thought to himself.

He followed the butterflies as they flitted from one sunny spot to the next.

But soon there was no more sunlight. The butterflies were gone. There was nothing but dark forest.

Oh dear, thought the littlest dinosaur. *It's not fun being small in the dark. But I have the heart of a dinosaur. I must be brave. If I walk back the way I came, I will find my way out of here.*

But which way had he come from? He had run this way and
that way following the butterflies and had lost all sense of
direction. The littlest dinosaur looked around. All the trees
looked the same – dark and spooky. The littlest dinosaur
was frightened. Birds and bats flew squawking into the sky.
Eyes watched from behind trees.

The littlest dinosaur ran. He tripped and slipped and stumbled through the dark forest until he was so tired he could run no further.

He crawled under the roots of a great tree and was just reminding himself that, with the heart of a dinosaur, he shouldn't cry, when he heard sobbing nearby. Looking around the back of the tree, the littlest dinosaur saw the oddest little creature he had ever seen.

"I am lost," cried
the little creature.

"Don't cry," the littlest dinosaur replied. "We'll be all right, you'll see."

He put his arm around the little creature and together they walked through the forest until the trees thinned and they could see the sky.

Suddenly it got very dark again
and a big, terrifying shape
swooped across the sky.

"Mummy!" cried the odd little creature. "Mummy!"
The little creature's mummy landed with a crash and folded her great wings around her baby. Then she looked at the littlest dinosaur. His knees trembled and his heart thumped.

"Come," the huge mummy said, "let's get you home."

With her baby and the littlest dinosaur clinging to her neck,
she beat her great wings and soared over the forest.
The littlest dinosaur pointed to the far river.

Soon they were circling over the amazed faces of the littlest dinosaur's family, who were all very happy to see him.

That night, snug in his bed, the littlest dinosaur dreamed
of his big adventure and of his new friends, big and small.
It had been a very exciting day!